the CRAZY world of PHOTOGRAPHY

Cartoons by
Bill Stott

EXLEY

MT. KISCO, NEW YORK • WATFORD, UK

"There you are Son: spot metering, focus confirmation, all the pieces ... Don't worry, Daddy will show you how to use it ..."

"Go home? You must be joking! But if you could get these developed and drop them off next time you're passing ..."

"That's cheating!"

"I name this child Agfa Minolta Nimslo Pratt!"

"*A flashgun? You* swallowed *a flashgun?!?!?*"

"*I think I preferred the days when it was a few cans of beer and a giggle at sports day snaps instead of white wine and 'Would you like to see my latest studies?'*"

"Who's been leaning over the wall then?"

"At least he's honest ..."

"You guys make me laugh if you don't mind me saying. I mean even Lord Wosisname says you can take super snaps wiv a pin and an old shoebox and there you are wiv all that stuff round yer necks ... Why don't you get one of those little jobs – just point and press and I'll bet my snaps are as good as yours ..."

"*Compliments of the opposing Commanders-in-Chief! Could you get a move on so that they can start killing each other?*"

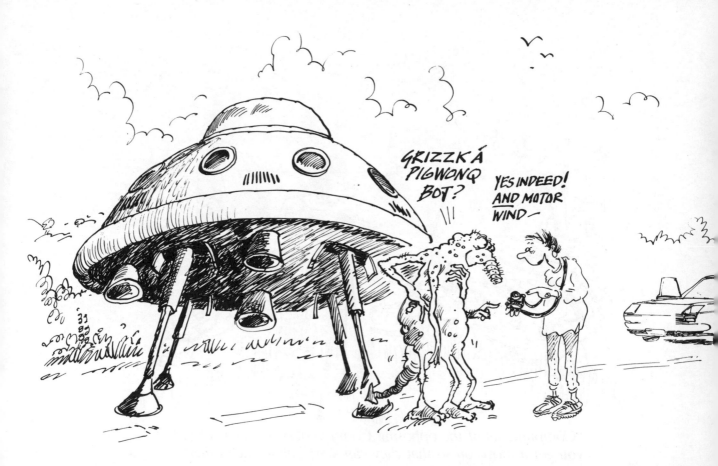

"*Heavens, look at the state of that neg! You've got a duff lens there, old man ...*"

"David – you must meet Fred – he's a camera bore, er buff, too ..."

*If their home-made wine is as bad as their photographs,
fake a head-ache and we'll make a break for it!"*

"And, for about the seventh time, I name this child ..."

"So, basically, it's a 35mm job with aperture priority, automatic
exposure with manual override and film plate TTL metering,
but the exposure compensations mechanism is
an absolute joy ..."

"Professional? Good lord, no! Wouldn't want to be part of that rat race ... Mind you I've taken some damn fine pictures if I do say so myself ... I remember once, when ..."

"Lesson 42: never point the flashgun at your face when 'the flash doesn't appear to be working' ..."

"May I suggest you jump from the other end? We're not going to get much against a setting sun ..."

"So I said to this enormous mugger 'I have every right to photograph street crime if I want to ...'"

"Oh there's nothing wrong with his legs; he's just too mean to buy a tripod!"

"*Take no notice. This month's craze is unusual angles....*"

"He wants you to move a little to the right ..."

"No don't tell me ... this button initiates focusing via the infra-red autofocus system (or, on some models, the contrast comparison method), then measures available light, sets the exposure and suggests built-in flash utilization. Right?"

"A fortune in technical virtuosity – a triumph of photographic genius – and he gets his finger stuck in it!"

"Listen! If my 98-year-old, doting, rich great-aunt knits you a camera case, you wear it – OK!?"

"Mmm ... They're very fuzzy –
er, atmospheric – aren't they?"

"*Now, do you believe there's such a thing as the too perfect hide?*"

"Has Mother's little soldier
been keeping nice and still
for the man?"

"Be patient – they'll be here. This is one of the most inconspicuous hides around."

"Good morning, young man! Have you ever seen a more perfect example of the Lesser Toadwort?"

"No darling, I wouldn't show them to Daddy – they're much better than his …"

"And this one marks the end of my 'Fascinating Faces' series."

"Of course with shy timid creatures, a good zoom is absolutely essential …"

"Nothing changes about putting a film in an obsolete Zenit –
even up here!"

*"I always do this for a couple of blocks with a new one –
I think a battered camera speaks volumes …"*

"Excuse me sir. I'm making a photographic record of truck drivers' secret gestures and signs. Would you mind if ..."

"Sometimes I don't know why we bother saying anything at all!"

"Fear not madam!
Thanks to my recently
acquired auto-wind,
this oaf doesn't stand
a chance!"

"So I said to this huge picket 'Listen Sunshine, this is a public highway and I'm a bona fide member of the press' ..."

"Look, I knew I'd seen it somewhere ... 'Do not dip your tie in this solution'."

"No instructions here either –
it just says 'Open other end' ..."

" ... so I feel a bit rejected ... Photography is gradually eroding our marriage ... we don't talk any more ... and WILL YOU PUT THAT THING DOWN WHEN I'M TALKING TO YOU!!?

"The light's not right?
What do you mean
'The light's not right'??"

"*And ambient metering is by cell in the viewfinder –flash metering too, so it's multi-mode. Synch speed on the dedicated flash to about 1/900, backlight button, quartz controlled manual shutter speed ... I'm not going too fast for you?*"

"Well, you don't get to be Sports Photographer of the Year by just hanging around on the touchline, you know!"

"Yes, it's good isn't it? I'm still trying to work out
what went wrong ..."

"And this is the one
when you came in and
said 'Remote control?
What remote control?'"

"Hmmn – dedicated zqiprtz, automatic ghzza'hq, but the wahqreeagh's not as advanced as ours ..."

"Sorry about this folks. Just a bit of professional sabotage from a rival photographer …"

Dear Sir

    My second-hand Niklax Z 200 recently developed a sticking shutter. I am told that this model is obsolete and I wondered if you could ✱ clarify a few points for me. When you take off the plate thing at the back and the spring flirts out and the little grub screws drop off onto the deep, shag-pile carpet, which way up should the semi-circular whatsname be? Also, I have re-assembled the camera a few times ✱ but I always seem to have several important-looking bits left...

"You received it as a gift, lost the instructions and can't find the little hole to look through? I'm not surprised; this is a personal stereo, Sir."

"It's very good of you to come out from town to judge our humble offerings ... Er, a word to the wise? The minister usually comes first as the vestry is also the darkroom ..."

"Of course that's an early one – before I got the hang of which end to look through ..."

"Excuse me. I wonder if you could move to your left? It would make a much more dramatic shot with the streetlight right behind you …"

"A message from our sponsor. He's brought the wrong film, so could you please take your foot off as you go past his billboard?"

"Well! All I can say is if they think anyone would send you as a spy, they must have some pretty ordinary secrets!"

"Photographic investigation of the supernatural demands high technical standards and patience, lots of patience ..."

"Okay! One last shot – and this time I wonder if the gentleman in the back row could put his hairpiece straight?"

"If you're such a hot-shot professional photographer, why are you pointing Sonya's radio at us?"

"And you're sure *you* remained unobserved throughout the whole operation, Crabtree?"

"Is this a dagger that I see before me?"
Or is it the idiot in the stalls with
a flashgun again?"

"My eye problem? Well, apparently it's due to persistent use of a wide-angle lens ..."

"See? And you wonder why I always keep my camera handy!"

"Why is it all blurred? Well – the indistinct outlines give the feeling of time passing, of fading reality – also someone jogged my elbow ..."

"Yes *I still love you*. Yes *I am enjoying the trip*. It's just that some pictures don't need people in them!"

"I may as well warn you now, so anyone wishing to leave can do so. My husband talks about nothing but cameras, film, enlargers, lenses and exposure times ..."

"*He's lousy with a camera, but an absolute ace on the enlarger …*"

"Excuse me. I'm making a personal photographic record of
spontaneous emotion and I wondered if you'd mind if ..."

"*Don't shout! It's kept him quiet all day!*"

"The customer says if it's dearer than the Japanese model, why
hasn't it got the wind-gauge, radio and compass?"

"He'll never be parted from his camera case."

"*Be with you in a minute. Gerald is still on his historical tableaux thing – we're doing the Storming of the Bastille this week!*"

"A photographer from the Health Department to see you, Sir."

"A simple 'No thank you' would have sufficed!"

"Don't panic! It says here 'If camera makes little moaning sounds and suddenly blows itself to pieces, consult your dealer'."

Books in the "Crazy World" series
($4.99 £2.99 paperback)

The Crazy World of Cats (Bill Stott)
The Crazy World of Cricket (Bill Stott)
The Crazy World of Gardening (Bill Stott)
The Crazy World of Golf (Mike Scott)
The Crazy World of the Greens (Barry Knowles)
The Crazy World of The Handyman (Roland Fiddy)
The Crazy World of Hospitals (Bill Stott)
The Crazy World of Housework (Bill Stott)
The Crazy World of Marriage (Bill Stott)
The Crazy World of The Office (Bill Stott)
The Crazy World of Photography (Bill Stott)
The Crazy World of Rugby (Bill Stott)
The Crazy World of Sailing (Peter Rigby)
The Crazy World of Sex (David Pye)

Books in the "Mini Joke Book" series
($6.99 £3.99 hardback)

These attractive 64 page mini joke books are illustrated throughout by Bill Stott.

A Binge of Diet jokes
A Bouquet of Wedding Jokes
A Feast of After Dinner Jokes
A Knockout of Sports Jokes
A Portfolio of Business Jokes
A Round of Golf Jokes
A Romp of Naughty Jokes
A Spread of Over-40s Jokes
A Tankful of Motoring Jokes

Books in the "Fanatics" series
($4.99 £2.99 paperback)

The **Fanatic's Guides** are perfect presents for everyone with a hobby that has got out of hand. Eighty pages of hilarious black and white cartoons by Roland Fiddy.

The Fanatic's Guide to the Bed
The Fanatic's Guide to Cats
The Fanatic's Guide to Computers
The Fanatic's Guide to Dads
The Fanatic's Guide to Diets
The Fanatic's Guide to Dogs
The Fanatic's Guide to Husbands
The Fanatic's Guide to Money
The Fanatic's Guide to Sex
The Fanatic's Guide to Skiing

Books in the "Victim's Guide" series
($4.99 £2.99 paperback)

Award winning cartoonist Roland Fiddy sees the funny side to life's phobias, nightmares and catastrophies.

The Victim's Guide to the Dentist
The Victim's Guide to the Doctor
The Victim's Guide to Middle Age

Great Britain: Order these super books from your local bookseller or From Exley Publications Ltd, 16 Chalk Hill, Watford, Herts WD1 4BN. (Please send £1.30 to cover postage and packing on 1 book, £2.60 on 2 or more books.)